This book belongs to

....

To all mums everywhere – especially Prim,
Louise, Sarah and Rebecca – J.M.

PUFFIN BOOKS
Published by the Penguin Group: London, New York,
Australia, Canada, India, Ireland, New Zealand and South Africa
Penguin Books Ltd, Registered Offices: 80 Strand, London WC2R 0RL, England
puffinbooks.com
First published 2011
001 – 10 9 8 7 6 5 4 3 2 1
Text and illustrations copyright © Jill Murphy, 2011
Made and printed in China
ISBN: 978–0–141–38411–5

Mother Knows Best!

Jill Murphy

PUFFIN

"Mu-u-um," said Bradley, "can I wear my pyjamas all day?"

"I think not," said Mum.

"*Why?*" asked Bradley.

"Pyjamas are for sleeping in," said Mum.

"But if I sleep in them," said Bradley, "no one ever sees them."

"*I* see them," said Mum, "and your dad sees them and so do you. That's quite a lot of people seeing you in your pyjamas, Bradley – *OK*?"

"OK," grumbled Bradley.

"**Mu-u-um**," asked Bradley, "can I have ice cream for breakfast?"

"No," said Mum, "you can't."

"*Why?*" asked Bradley.

"Because you have to have sensible stuff for breakfast," said Mum. "That's why."

"Cakes are sensible," said Bradley. "I could have cakes instead and then –"

"It's porridge for breakfast, Bradley," said Mum. "*OK?*"

"OK," agreed Bradley.

"Mu-u-um," said Bradley, "can I have a pet dinosaur?"

"No chance," said Mum.

"Why not?" asked Bradley.

"Because they're extinct," said Mum, "that's why."

"What does 'extinct' mean?" asked Bradley.

"It means there aren't any," said Mum. "*OK?*"

"OK," said Bradley.

"*Mu-u-um,*"

said Bradley, "can bears fly?"

"I don't think so, darling," said Mum.

"I might just have a little try," said Bradley.

"Don't try it on the sofa," called Mum.

"*Why not?*" asked Bradley.

"Because you might fall off," called Mum, "and –"

THUD!

"– hurt yourself. Come on, let's have a cuddle and a calm down."

"*Mu-u-um,*" said Bradley.

"Enough questions for a while, darling," said Mum. "*I* know!
Why don't you watch TV for a bit? There's a nice programme on
right now, it's one that you like."

So Mum switched on the TV and Bradley plonked himself down in the big chair and watched his programme and had a little snooze while Mum got the lunch ready.

"*Mu-u-um*," said Bradley, "can I go up in a hot-air balloon?"

"Of course you can't, darling!" laughed Mum.

"Why not?" asked Bradley.

"Too dangerous," said Mum. "You might fall out of the basket. Oh, for goodness' sake, Bradley, this is ridiculous – you just can't, *OK*?"

"*OK*," said Bradley.

"**Mu-u-um,**" said Bradley, "can I watch some *more* TV?"

"I'd rather you didn't," said Mum,
"there are better things to do
than watch TV all day."

"What things?" asked Bradley.

"Well," said Mum, "you could play with your toys, or draw me a nice picture."

"I'll draw you a boat," said Bradley.

"Thanks," said Mum, "that would be lovely."

"I've done your picture, Mum," said Bradley.
"Do you like it?"

"I love it," said Mum.

"*Mu-u-um,*" said Bradley, "can we *make* a boat for me to play in?"

"Good idea," said Mum.

They put the boat in the middle of the room and Mum put cushions round it.

"The cushions are sharks," said Mum. "You'd better stay in the boat or the sharks will get you – *OK?*"

"COOL!" said Bradley.

"Mu-u-um," said Bradley. "I've killed all the sharks – can we make some pancakes?"

"I'd rather we didn't," said Mum.

"Why not?" asked Bradley.

"Because I just can't face it," said Mum, "that's why."

"But *you* said I should be doing things," said Bradley. "*You* said it's better to do things than watch TV."

"*OK*," said Mum. "Let's make the pancakes."

"Mu-u-um," said Bradley, "when it's bedtime, can I stay up all night?"

"*Not* a good idea," said Mum.

"Why not?" asked Bradley.

"Well," said Mum, "it would be a bit silly if you were running about all night when your dad and I had gone to bed."

"But, Mum –" said Bradley.

"That's enough now," said Mum.
"*I* know! Let's go to the park
and you can play on the swings."

"Mu-u-um," said Bradley, "can I go to the park by myself?"

"GIVE ME STRENGTH," said Mum.

"Why?" asked Bradley.

"Never mind," said Mum. "You're just too young to go out by yourself."

"But *why*?" asked Bradley.

"I've just *TOLD* you!" said Mum. "It's because you're too young to go out by yourself – and because you might get lost – and there are roads to cross and it's because … because …

"*OK?*" said Mum.

"OK," said Bradley.

And off they went to
the park – together.

"Mu-u-um..."

The End